SHY MAMA'S HALLOWEEN

Anne Broyles

Illustrated by Leane Morin

Tilbury House, Publishers • Gardiner, Maine

"But I don't know this — this Halloween," Mama protested.

"Come with us, Mama. Please." All four of us stood before her, pleading in our eyes. Halloween was new for us, too, but we knew we didn't want to miss it.

Our first chance for Halloween! Back home in the old country, there was no Halloween. Vas'movo, yes. Pyervova Maya, yes. But no Halloween.

Like so much of life in America, Halloween frightened Mama. When she heard us tell of ghosts and goblins, witches and spirits, she wanted no part of this holiday.

Even in the old country, Mama was shy. So I was not surprised when she said, "Your father can do this trick-or-treat with you."

There was no equivalent in our language for "trick or treat." The Halloween vocabulary fell clumsily from Mama's lips. I could tell that she was grateful our father would be the one to help us know Halloween when we went on the trick-or-treat for the first time in our lives. Our father knew English from his job in the old country, and he had visited the United States once before we immigrated here. Besides, as Mama said, Papa was more adventurous.

Mrs. Rumanski, our upstairs neighbor, helped Mama make our costumes.

Mrs. R worked in a dress shop and brought home remnants of fabric that, under

her magic fingers, were transformed into Halloween wonders on her midnight-blue

Singer sewing machine.

Dasha was a princess, of course. The jewels in her silver crown matched the pink velvet of her royal cape, which swished all the way down to the floor.

It was no surprise that Dimitrii wanted to be a clown. In his polka-dotted suit and red, curly wig, my little brother looked quite entertaining.

When Irina appeared in her black outfit, we all gasped. The pointed witch's hat and papier-mâché nose changed her sweet face into something frightening and strange. I was not sure how I felt seeing my little sister as a wicked enchantress.

I liked being a devil because my favorite color is red. The satiny feel of my suit made me forget I was supposed to be bad until I felt the strength of the pitchfork in my hands. No one would bother me!

And so, on Halloween night, we got into our costumes and waited for Papa to come home from work to take us on the trick-or-treat.

Mama fussed over us to eat more dinner, but we were too excited. Dasha could not stop talking.

Dimitrii was the opposite and sat with his finger in his mouth, eyes wide, a somber clown.

We looked at the clock. "Where is Papa? Will he come soon?" It was getting dark outside. Shrieks of laughter mixed with joyous cries of "Trick or treat!" from the neighborhood children as they passed by our building.

The clock ticked on. Still no Papa. Would we ever get to do the trick-or-treat? Mama seemed alarmed by the noise outside. She would be happy to stay cozy inside the apartment, away from the hustle and bustle of the Halloween crowd.

When Papa finally came through the door, our faces fell. "You are sick, Stefan!" Mama cried, and hurried him off to bed with a hot drink for his sore throat.

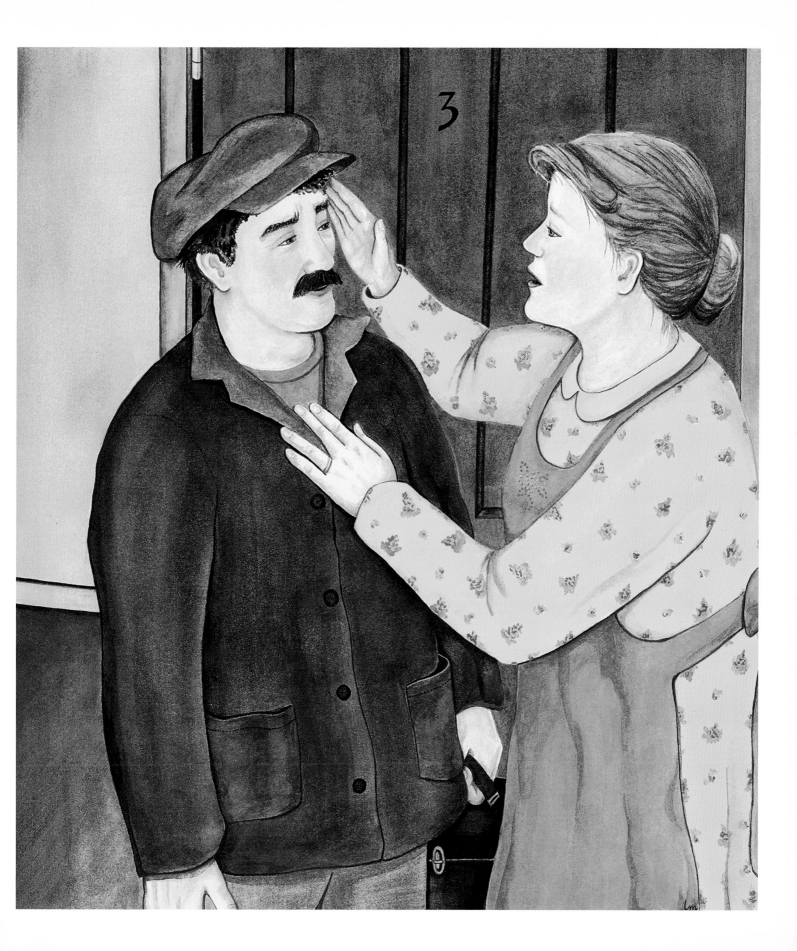

Outside, on the busy street, Halloween happened without us. I felt a sudden sense of longing for the familiarity of my old home. Who cared about a silky red devil's jacket and a silly pitchfork?

We children sat by the window, looking down to the busy street below. Mickey Mouse, Superman, witches all danced through the street past us. It was a party!

And now, with Papa sick, we were going to miss it. Dimitrii leaned close to me and began to cry wordlessly.

"Hush, Mitya. There will be other Halloweens." I stroked his curly red wig. "Papa cannot help being sick. And Mama cannot help being shy." I sighed, gazing out the window, and repeated, not very convincingly, "There will be other Halloweens."

"Are you ready, my children?"

We couldn't believe our eyes. Mama stood behind us, flashlight in hand.
"It is time we go." Her babushka was tied under her chin, her winter coat
firmly buttoned.

"Well, have you decided not to go?"

"Oh, no!" and we were up in an instant: princess, witch, devil, clown.

We raced down the stairs, eager to meet the cold of the air outside.

We followed the crowd, walking towards the neighborhood with the big houses. Carved jack-o'-lanterns greeted us from every porch. Groups of children bustled from house to house, parading their bright costumes and collecting bags full of goodies.

"Only in America," Mama said again and again. "Free treats to strangers!"

Everyone on the street was our friend, it seemed, though we could not tell who was who behind the masks. I liked the friendly feel of this Halloween.

Although the air was brisk, Dasha soon got tired of the weight of her royal robe. Mama slung it around her shoulders. The pink of the robe reflected her rosy cheeks.

Soon our bags felt heavy with treasures to eat. Dimitrii was tired, his small legs weary from so much walking. I handed Mama my devil's pitchfork so I could carry him.

"Haven't we had fun, Dimitrii?" I was glad we hadn't ended Halloween with tears by the window. My brother relaxed into my chest, his red wig slipping down over his eyes until I gave it to Mama.

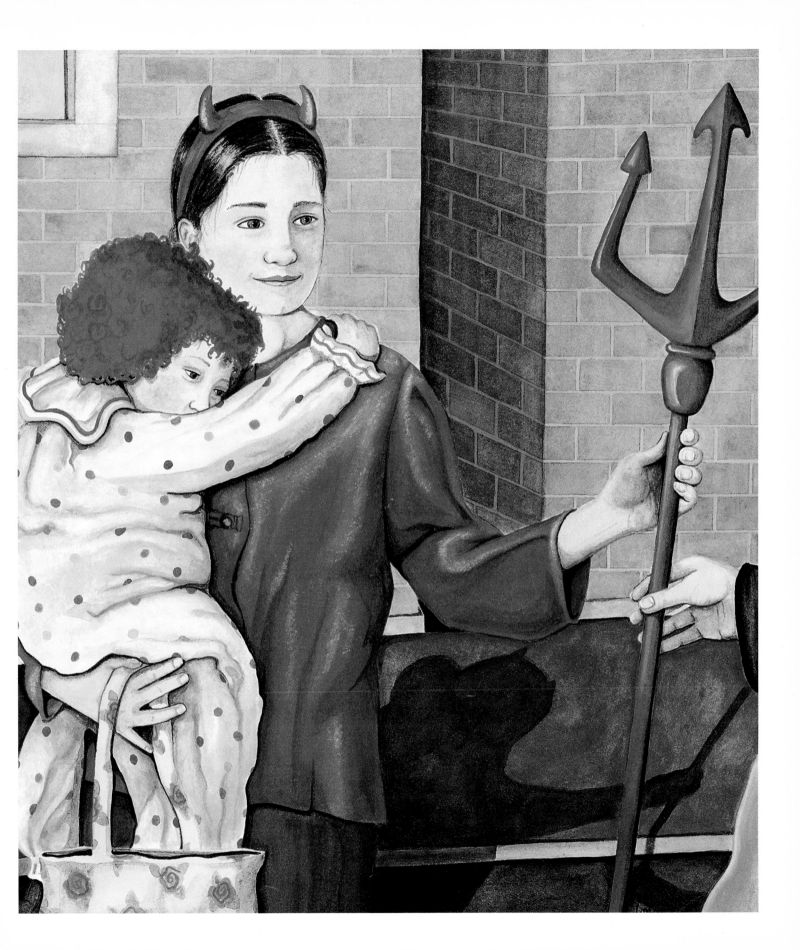

Things were different this night. I had walked down this street before, but tonight it was a magical path whose wonders I could not predict. Irina the Witch seemed even spookier in the darkness lit only by porch lights and the glow of jack-o'-lanterns' teeth. I was glad when she took off her tall hat and handed it to Mama to carry.

"Shall we go back now?"

Mama's question was met with our quick response, "No, not yet!"

We didn't need more fruit or cookies or candy. We already had more treats in our bags than we had had in a lifetime. We wanted to savor the magic of Halloween: its orange and blackness, the sounds of happy children, the smiles on adult faces as they surveyed the variety of trick-or-treating creatures, the chirps of "Thank you! Happy Halloween!" as kings and monsters raced away from the generous hands outstretched with candy.

Halloween was not just a matter of treats. We had no tricks in mind. Here, in the darkness, surrounded by what seemed like hundreds of other children, we, too, were American. No one cared that our "Thank you" was said with an accent. No one cared that our Mama, in her babushka, could speak only a few words of English. Halloween was our holiday, as much as anyone else's.

All too soon, though, my arms were weary from Dimitrii's weight.

"I'm tired," Dasha complained. Even Irina the Witch was slowing down.

Mama asked gently, "Do you think it is time to go home now?"

We all nodded, contented.

We walked slowly back to the apartment. Mama hummed one of our country's songs, her arms draped around Dasha's and Irina's shoulders as we made our way home. Still carrying Dimitrii, I followed behind the three of them, eager to get home and count my goodies piece by piece. Surely there were at least a million treats in my bag!

Up we went to our own cozy place. I laid Dimitrii in his bed. He would have polka-dot pajamas this night. And who knew what creatures would fill his dreams?

"One treat and then to bed," Mama told us. "And don't forget to brush your teeth."

Wearily, we girls crowded around the sink. Mama came up behind us and when I saw her reflection in the mirror, I stopped my toothbrush before it reached my mouth.

Our shy Mama stood behind us. Her winter coat was hidden by the velvety folds of a princess robe. Over her babushka sat a red, curly wig on which precariously balanced Irina's witch's hat, black against red.

Mama stood in strength, my devil's pitchfork grasped firmly in her hand. But it was the look in her eyes that amazed me as she gazed steadily at the Mama-in-the-mirror.

My shy Mama's eyes sparkled, happier than I had seen her since we made the big move to a faraway country where she felt a stranger. My glance met those sparkling eyes in the mirror, and all I could do was say happily, "Oh, Mama!"

"Now, Anya," she replied, sounding serious and joyful at the same time, "Now I know this Halloween," and sighed with pleasure.

Sharing SHY MAMA'S HALLOWEEN with Children — Suggestions for Parents and Teachers

MOVING TO A NEW HOME

Immigrant: A person who comes to a new country to make a new home.

Sometimes people leave their homes and move to another country because they are fleeing persecution or war, or because they are hoping for a better job and a better way of life. Countries like the United States and Canada have long histories of immigration. Between 1892 and 1954, for instance, 12 million people passed through America's Ellis Island immigration station in New York Harbor. There are many immigrants who have gone to other countries in all parts of the world.

It always takes courage to immigrate to a new land. For many people, the journey can be frightening, taking weeks of travel in sometimes unpleasant conditions. Some immigrants have to pass a physical examination and answer questions about themselves before they are allowed to enter another country. And always, in the immigrants' minds, there are questions like: What will my new country be like? Will we find a place to live? Will people welcome us? Will we make friends?

Anya's family made a big move from their native Russia. Everything was new for them, including Halloween. After you read *Shy Mama's Halloween*, here are some questions to explore.

THINKING ABOUT ANYA'S LIFE

Imagine what it would have felt like to come to a new country where the language, customs, culture, and traditions were new and different from what you knew.

• Find Russia, Anya's old country, on a globe or world map.
• Even though Mama was shy and spoke very little English, she took her children "to do the trick or treat." Why?
• Look at Mama's face on the cover of *Shy Mama's Halloween.* How do you think she is feeling and why? Now look at Mama's face at the end of the story, when she is looking at herself in the mirror. How has her expression changed? Why do you think it has?
• The illustrator gives us other visual clues about Anya's family and their lives. Look at the pictures. What do the illustrations tell you about Anya? Irina? Dasha? Dimitrii? Papa? Mama? What are they like? Can you think of words to describe this family?
• How would Anya and her sisters and brother have managed at school and in their neighborhood as they were just learning English?
• Papa seemed to feel at home more quickly than Mama did in the new country. Can you think of some reasons why?
• On the last page of the story Mama says to Anya, "Now I know this Halloween." What do you think she means by that? Do you think she's talking just about Halloween night?

THINKING ABOUT YOUR LIFE

Even though *Shy Mama's Halloween* took place years ago, experiencing immigration or any big change today is still exciting and challenging.

• Have you ever moved or do you know someone who has? How do you think it feels to be in a new school—neighborhood—country?

• What would be some good experiences a person could have on his or her first day at a new school? What could be some bad ones? How could you help someone new in your class feel more at home and welcome? How could you and your family welcome a new person or family into your neighborhood or building?

• Are there children at your school who originally came from other countries as immigrants? Look up where they came from on a world map or globe. Can you give these classmates a chance to tell you about the places where they came from? What do they miss about their old home? What do they like about their new home? Who or what helped them feel comfortable in their new home?

• How would you feel if someone made fun of the way you dressed, looked, or spoke? What could you do about it? What could you do to help if you heard someone making fun of another child?

• Mama was led out into the world by her children's desire to be part of Halloween. What have you discovered on your own that helped your parent(s) or a grown-up try something new?

• Do you think grown-ups feel frightened when they move or begin a new job? Interview a grown-up you know and ask him or her to tell you about how it feels to face a change or new experience.

HALLOWEEN AND OTHER TRADITIONS

When people move to a new country, they often bring their own traditions and holidays with them. Halloween is a holiday that originated with Celtic people in Ireland, Scotland, and England. Some think that Halloween is a combination of the pagan Celtic holiday "Samhain," and the Christian All Souls' Day. Samhain was celebrated on October 31, the last day of the Celtic year, as the end of summer and a festival of the dead. All Souls' Day (or Allhallows Eve) is also observed on October 31 in preparation for All Saints' Day on November 1. Where does trick or treating come from? There was an old Irish practice of going from house to house to beg for food and gifts in preparation for Halloween parties. In some places, on All Souls' Day the poor would go from house to house to beg for sweet cakes, promising to say prayers for the dead in return. In Scotland in the mid 1800s youngsters would go in costume to seek treats. This was known as "guising."

• Are there other holidays we celebrate that come from traditions in other countries? The two Russian holidays mentioned on the first page of the book are Vas'movo, which is an international women's day celebrated on March 8 when children give flowers as gifts to mothers and grandmothers and other women, and Pyervova Maya, a celebration of spring on the first of May.

• What are some traditions that your family observes? Are they traditions that have been passed down, or are they new traditions started in your lifetime?

• Could you make up a new holiday that celebrates all the different kinds of people who come to our country? What would you call it? What would this holiday be like?

For additional activities using *Shy Mama's Halloween*, along with some suggestions for further reading, please visit our web site at www.tilburyhouse.com

Special thanks to Leane Morin, Diane Vinal, and Rachel Deblois for their help with these two pages.

For Trinity and Justus; written in the hope that there will always be welcome in the United States for immigrants and their unique perspective. —A. B.

For my wonderful children, Katherine, Samuel, and Margaret. Special thanks to Diane, Genny, Buster, and the Tilbury House Family for all their help and support. —L. M.

Tilbury House, Publishers • 2 Mechanic Street • Gardiner, ME 04345
800–582–1899

First Printing: August 2000.

10 9 8 7 6 5 4 3 2 1

Library of Congress Cataloging-in-Publication Data

Broyles, Anne, 1953-
       Shy Mama's Halloween / Anne Broyles; illustrations by Leane Avery Morin.
       p. cm.
       Summary: When their father gets sick and cannot take them out trick or treating on their first Halloween in their new country, Anya and her sisters and brother are surprised when their shy mother agrees to accompany them.
       ISBN 0-88448-218-9 (alk. paper)
       [1. Halloween—Fiction. 2. Immigrants—Fiction. 3. Family life—Fiction.] I. Morin, Leane Avery, ill. II. Title.

PZ7.B82447 Sh 2000
[E]—dc21   00-039225

Design by Geraldine Millham, Westport, Massachusetts.
Color separations and film by Integrated Composition Systems, Spokane, Washington.
Printing and binding by Worzalla Publishing, Stevens Point, Wisconsin.